Dear Parent:
Your child's love of reading

Every child learns to read in a different way and at his or her own speed. Some go back and forth between reading levels and read favorite books again and again. Others read through each level in order. You can help your young reader improve and become more confident by encouraging his or her own interests and abilities. From books your child reads with you to the first books he or she reads alone, there are I Can Read Books for every stage of reading:

SHARED READING
Basic language, word repetition, and whimsical illustrations, ideal for sharing with your emergent reader

BEGINNING READING
Short sentences, familiar words, and simple concepts for children eager to read on their own

READING WITH HELP
Engaging stories, longer sentences, and language play for developing readers

READING ALONE
Complex plots, challenging vocabulary, and high-interest topics for the independent reader

ADVANCED READING
Short paragraphs, chapters, and exciting themes for the perfect bridge to chapter books

I Can Read Books have introduced children to the joy of reading since 1957. Featuring award-winning authors and illustrators and a fabulous cast of beloved characters, I Can Read Books set the standard for beginning readers.

A lifetime of discovery begins with the magical words **"I Can Read!"**

Visit www.icanread.com for information
on enriching your child's reading experience.

GOING TO THE SEA PARK

BY MERCER MAYER

HARPER
An Imprint of HarperCollinsPublishers

To Winkie and Wadam

I Can Read Book® is a trademark of HarperCollins Publishers.

Library of Congress catalog card number: 2009925074
ISBN 978-0-06-083554-5 (trade bdg.) — ISBN 978-0-06-083553-8 (pbk.)

Typography by Sean Boggs
09 10 11 12 13 LP/WOR   10 9 8 7 6 5 4 3   ❖   First Edition

 A Big Tuna Trading Company, LLC/J. R. Sansevere Book
www.littlecritter.com

Today my class goes
to the Sea Park.
It has so many fish.

There are little fish.

There are big fish.

Some fish are pretty.

Some fish are really ugly.

We all go to the petting tank.

I pet a horseshoe crab.
That is weird!

13

Timothy falls
into the tank.

He meets an octopus.
He is not happy.

I wish I could meet an octopus!

Our teacher takes us
to the lunchroom.

They sell a swordfish
burger on the menu.
I want that.

We go on a
pretend pirate ship.

I steer the ship.

Bun Bun is scared.

After lunch,
we see the shark tank.

I would not like to have lunch with a shark.

We see baby whales
eating fish.

We see manatees
eating plants.

Next we go to the seal show.

I feed a fish to a seal.

No one else wants to.

We see Bazoo the orca.

We sit in the front row.

We get splashed with water.
I am all wet!

Everyone brings money
from home to buy a gift.

Gator buys a seal.

Tiger gets a shark.

I buy a fuzzy orca.

What a great day we had
at the Sea Park.

30

Do you know
what the best part was?

Getting all wet!